3

Mum sees Rat.

Mum sees Rat.

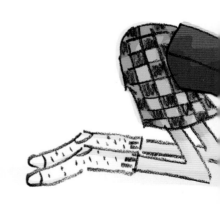

Mum sees Rat.

9

Mum sees Rat.

11

Mum sees Rat.

13

Mum sees Rat.

Mum sees Rat.

17

Mum sees Rat.

Story trail

Start at the beginning of the story trail. Ask your child to retell the story in their own words, pointing to each picture in turn to recall the sequence of events.

Start

Independent Reading

This series is designed to provide an opportunity for your child to read on their own. These notes are written for you to help your child choose a book and to read it independently.

In school, your child's teacher will often be using reading books which have been banded to support the process of learning to read. Use the book band colour your child is reading in school to help you make a good choice. *Mum Sees Rat* is a good choice for children reading at Pink 1a in their classroom to read independently.

The aim of independent reading is to read this book with ease, so that your child enjoys the story and relates it to their own experiences.

About the book
Rat has escaped from his cage and Mum keeps seeing him everywhere! Luckily, Anna is on hand to get him back.

Before reading
Help your child to learn how to make good choices by asking: "Why did you choose this book? Why do you think you will enjoy it?" Look at the cover together and ask: "What do you think the story will be about?" Support your child to think about what they already know about keeping small pets. "Where do pet rats go to sleep?" Read the title aloud and ask: "Why might Mum see Rat? What has happened?" Remind your child that they can try to sound out the letters to make a word if they get stuck.

Decide together whether your child will read the story independently or read it aloud to you. When books are short, as at Pink 1a, your child may wish to do both!

During reading

If reading aloud, support your child if they hesitate or ask for help by telling the word. Remind your child of what they know and what they can do independently.

If reading to themselves, remind your child that they can come and ask for your help if stuck.

After reading:

Support understanding of the story by asking your child to tell you what the story is about.

Help your child think about the messages in the book that go beyond the story and ask: "Do you think that Mum could have caught the rat and put him back in his cage? Why/why not?"

Give your child a chance to respond to the story: "Did you have a favourite part? What would you do if you had a pet that kept escaping from its cage?"

Use the story trail to encourage your child to retell the story in the right sequence, in their own words.

Extending learning

Help your child understand the story structure by using the same sentence structure with a different animal to make a new story. A pet parrot who has escaped outside (Mum sees Parrot) or a monkey who has escaped from the zoo (Mum sees Monkey), for example.

Your child's teacher will be encouraging accurate finger pointing at Pink 1a. Help your child learn to recognise and find commonly used words. Ask them to point to each of the words in turn on each page, starting with *Mum* and then *Rat* as these words are the easiest to find.

Franklin Watts
First published in Great Britain in 2017
by The Watts Publishing Group

Series Editors: Jackie Hamley and Melanie Palmer
Series Advisors: Dr Sue Bodman and Glen Franklin
Series Designer: Peter Scoulding

A CIP catalogue record for this book is
available from the British Library.

ISBN 978 1 4451 5401 5 (hbk)
ISBN 978 1 4451 5402 2 (pbk)

Printed in China

Franklin Watts
An imprint of
Hachette Children's Group
Part of The Watts Publishing Group
Carmelite House
50 Victoria Embankment
London EC4Y 0DZ

An Hachette UK Company
www.hachette.co.uk

www.franklinwatts.co.uk